Claire Bond lives in Cornwall and enjoys exploring the coastline and countryside. She loves animals, both wild and domestic. Her hobbies include art, photography, writing, music, films and sport.

Claire is a primary school teacher with a curriculum specialism in art and design. She has a love of literacy through teaching, books and films. As a kid she enjoyed reading fairy tales, comics and watching cartoons.

She was inspired to write picture book stories when she became a mummy. Having experienced first-hand the excitement and curiosity of little one's approach to the world, Claire's inner child and imagination was sparkled too!

MY PET ZEBRA

Claire Bond

AUSTIN MACAULEY PUBLISHERS™

LONDON • CAMBRIDGE • NEW YORK • SHARJAH

A CIP catalogue record for this title is available from the British Library.

ISBN 9781528911153 (Paperback)
ISBN 9781398423497 (ePub e-book)

www.austinmacauley.com

First Published 2022
Austin Macauley Publishers Ltd®
1 Canada Square
Canary Wharf
London
E14 5AA

There was a girl, called Claire, who had a pet zebra.
One morning, Claire was getting ready to
go out for a ride on her zebra.

"What will we see on our ride?" asked Claire.
Off they went. Clippity clop, clippity clop!

First, they saw a farmer driving his big, red tractor.
Brrm, brrm!

Then, they saw sheep in a grassy field.Baa, baa!
"I can see one, two, three, four, five sheep,"
said Claire.

Suddenly, Claire spotted something on top of a hill in the distance.

"I wonder what that is?" said Claire.

Claire and zebra galloped off up the hill. Clippity clop, clippity clop!

They came across an enormous red and white striped tent. It was a travelling circus.

There were circus performers practising.
Some balanced balls brilliantly.
Some juggled jokingly.
Some towered terribly tall!

Claire heard the ringmaster talking to a boy. "Sorry Max, your horse tricks act will have to be cancelled because your horse is not well," said the ringmaster.

Claire had an idea...

"Can we help? My pet zebra and I can learn the act," said Claire.

"Yes, I can teach you the tricks," said Max. "That's a great idea! Claire and zebra can perform in the circus show," agreed the ringmaster.

Step by step, Max trained Claire and zebra each daring trick. It was difficult at first. The tricks got easier the more they practised.

Eventually, they had learnt the whole act.
"Super effort working together as a team!" said Max.

Soon the circus show would start. It was time to get ready.

Inside a small tent were different circus costumes. "What shall I wear?" asked Claire.

Claire loved dressing up. She wore a pretty dress and a feathery tiara.

Suddenly, loud exciting music played.
The 3o'clock show had begun.

"Ladies and gentlemen, boys and girls, the amazing Claire and her pet zebra!" announced the ringmaster.

First, Claire rode in sitting bare back. Clippity clop, clippity clop!

Next, she stood up on top of zebra's back, cantering around the ring. The crowd cheered and clapped as they performed the terrific tricks.

Finally, Claire waved farewell to the audience. Then off they went out of the enormous tent. Clippity clop, clippity clop!

Eventually, the fantastic circus show had finished. It was a great success.

As a thank you, the ringmaster gave Claire the beautiful tiara to keep.

"Wow, we've had an amazing ride today! Now it's time to go home," said Claire.